Author Frances Díaz Evans
Illustrator Alejandra López

ISBN: 9798846466517
Imprint: Independently published

Autora Frances Díaz Evans
Ilustradora Alejandra López

Este libro de colorear le pertenece a
This coloring book belongs to

____

Sol, nubes y aves
Sun, clouds and birds

Bosque tropical El Yunque
Tropical Rainforest El Yunque

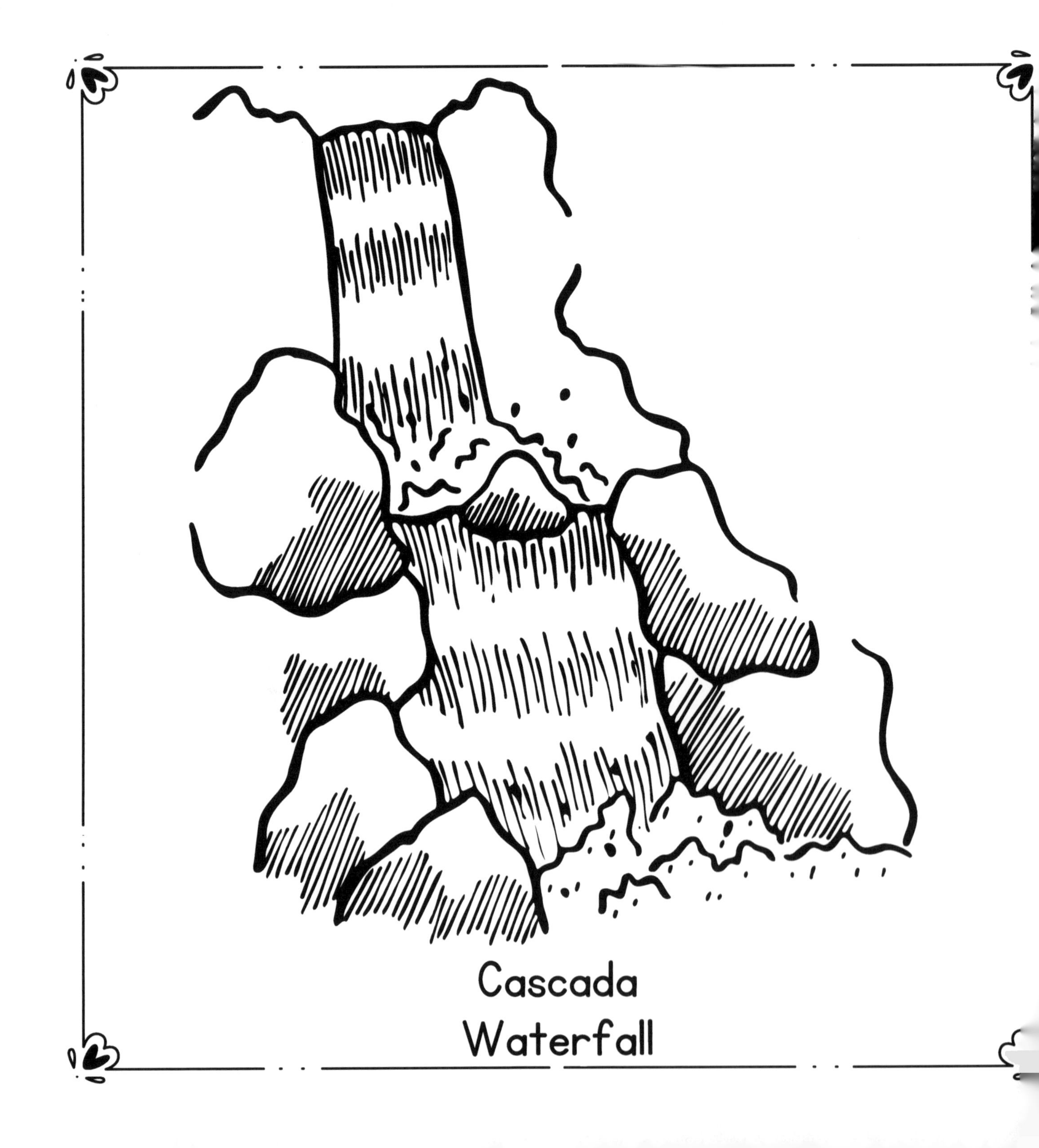
Cascada
Waterfall

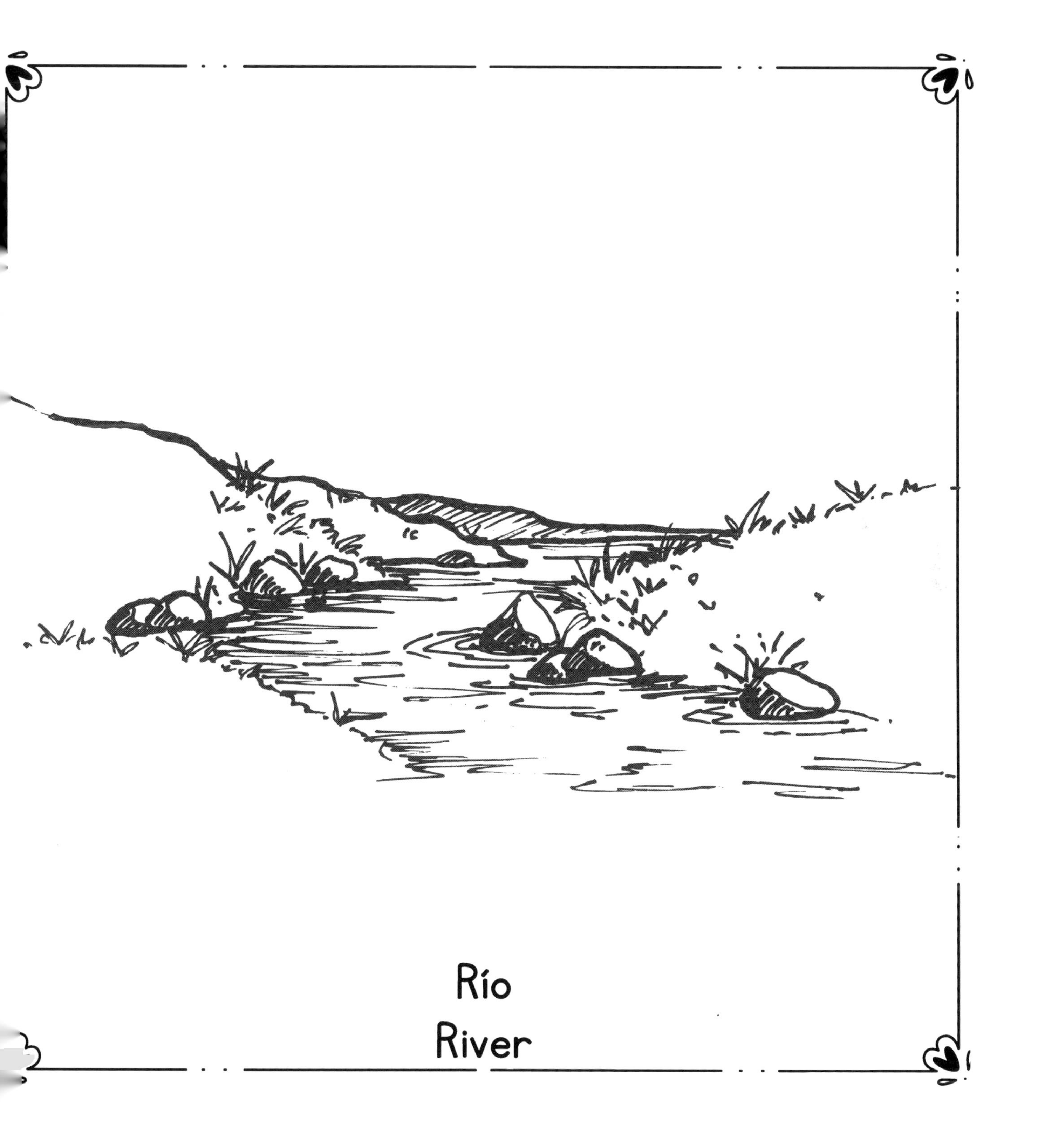

Río
River

Fran la avicultora
Fran the aviculturist

Leo the boy

Leo el niño

Aves
Birds

Coco la cotorra
Coco the parrot

Aves
Birds
Caimito la cotorra
Caimito the parrot
Cotorra puertorriqueña
Puerto Rican Parrot

Aves
Birds
Carambola la cotorra
Carambola the parrot
Cotorra de la Hispaniola
Hispaniolan Parrot

Aves
Birds

Reina mora
Puerto Rico Spindalis

Aves
Birds
Comeñame
Puerto Rican Bullfinch

Aves
Birds

San Pedrito
Puerto Rican Tody

Aves
Birds

Guaraguao halcón de cola roja
Red-tailed Hawk

Anfibios
Amphibians

Coquí común
Common Coqui

Reptiles

Reptiles

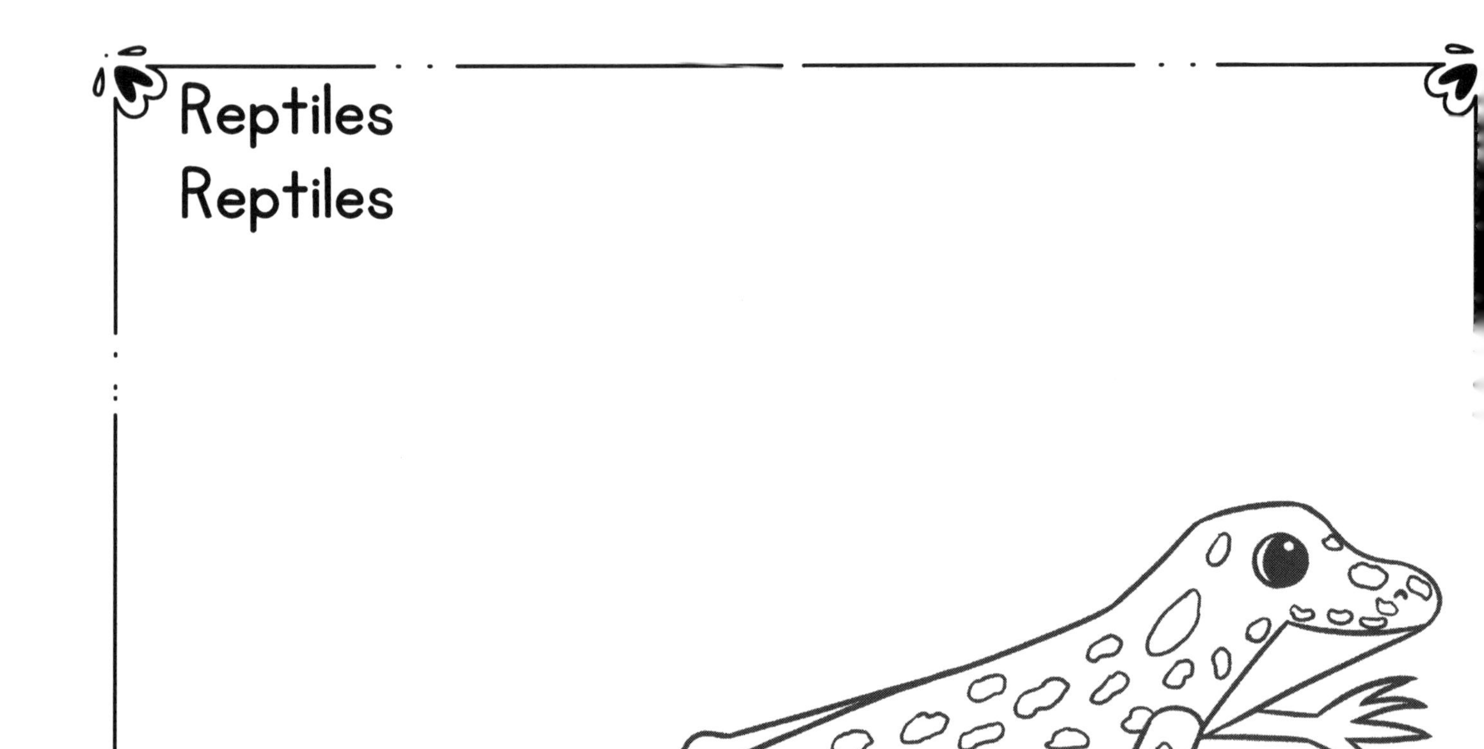

Lagartijo común

Puerto Rican Crested Anole (Lizard)

Reptiles
Reptiles

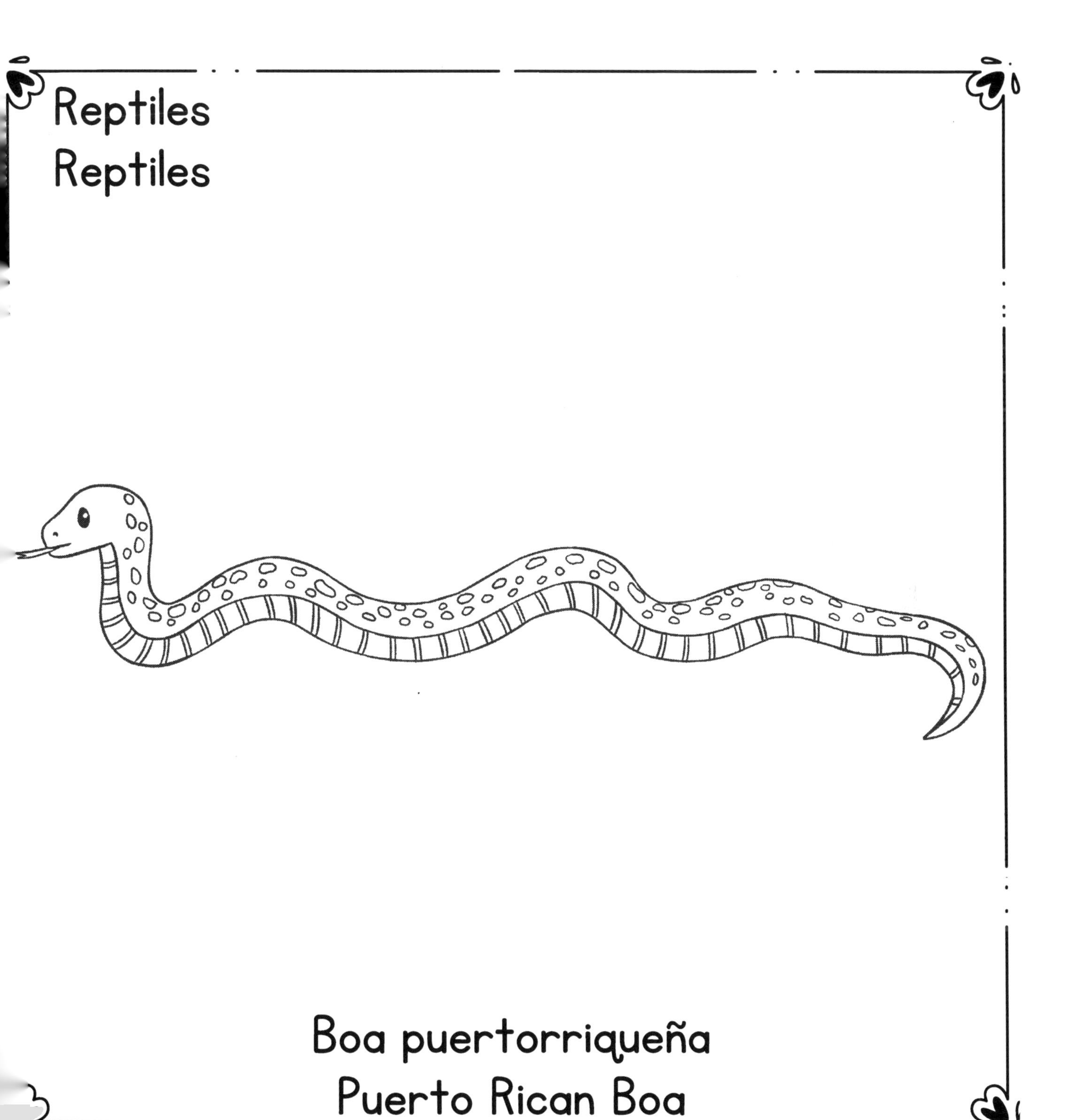

Boa puertorriqueña
Puerto Rican Boa

Flora
(Flowers, Plants & Trees)

Flora
(Flores, plantas y árboles)

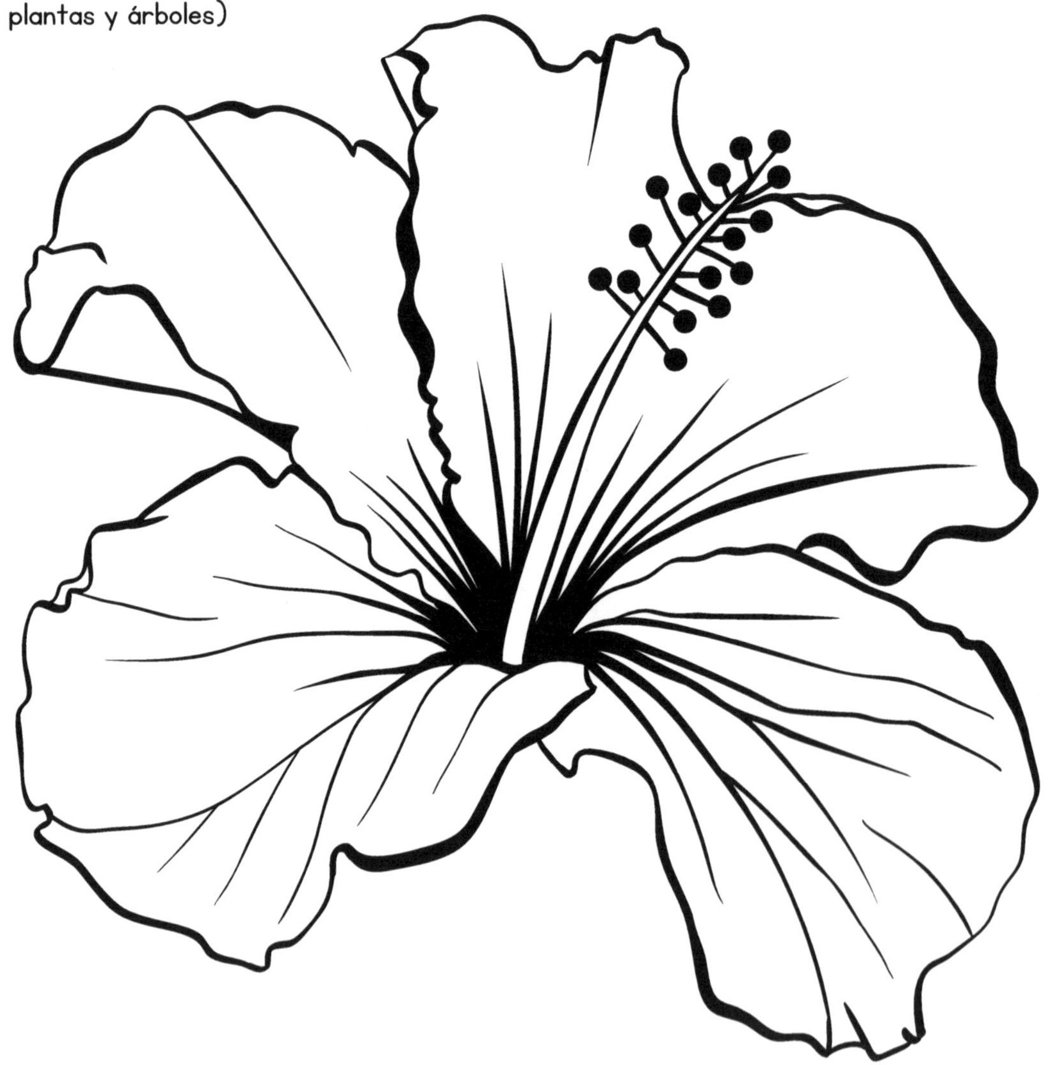

Flor de maga

Flower of the maga tree

Flora
(Flowers, Plants & Trees)
Flora
(Flores, plantas y árboles)
Hoja de ortiga brava
Stinging Nettle Leaf

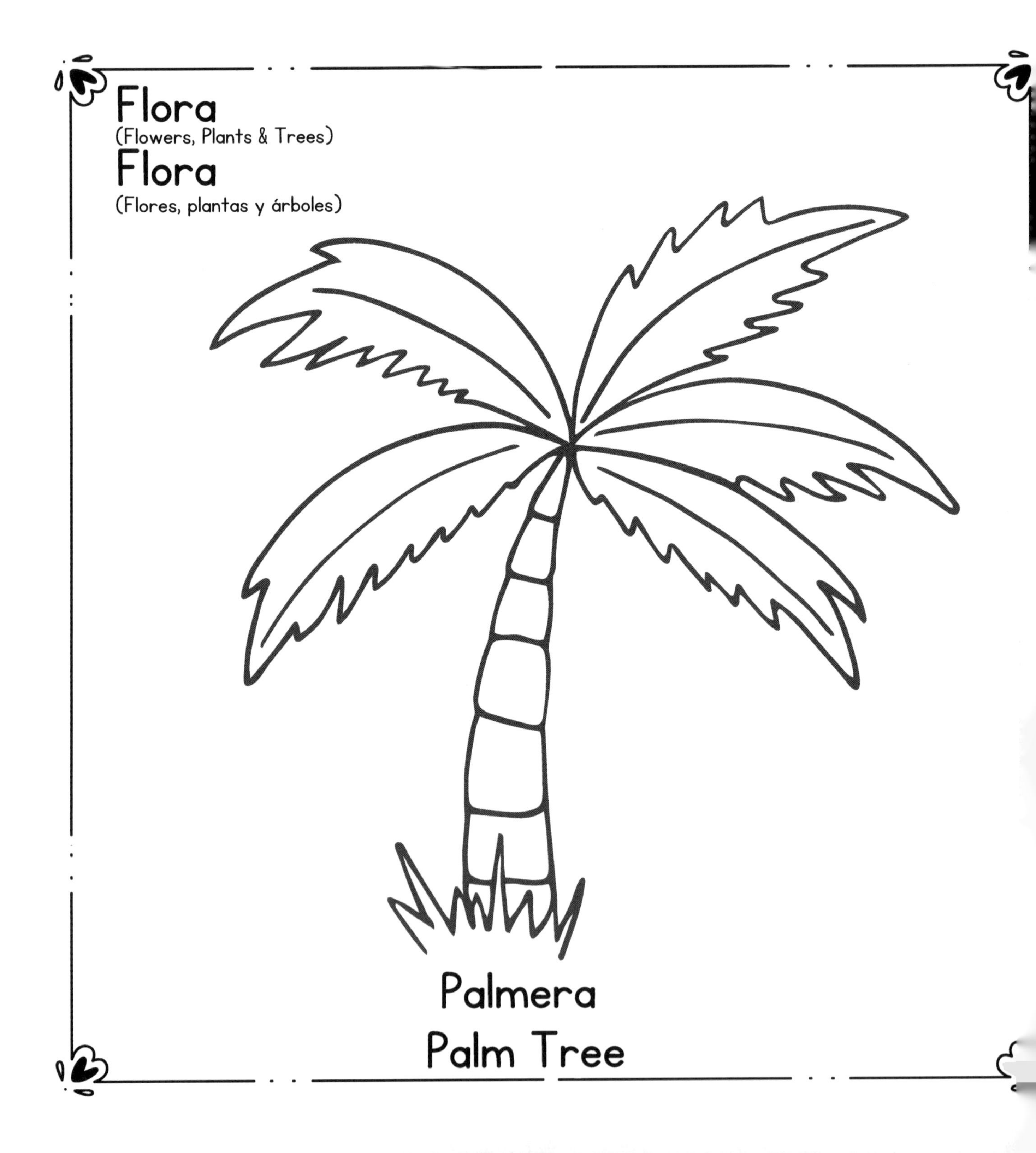
Flora
(Flowers, Plants & Trees)
Flora
(Flores, plantas y árboles)
Palmera
Palm Tree

Flora
(Flowers, Plants & Trees)
Flora
(Flores, plantas y árboles)
Hojas de palma
Palm leaves

Flora
(Flowers, Plants & Trees)
Flora
(Flores, plantas y árboles)

Árbol de yagrumo
Trumpet-tree

Flora
(Flowers, Plants & Trees)
Flora
(Flores, plantas y árboles)

Hojas de yagrumo

Trumpet-tree (yagrum) leaves

Flora
(Flowers, Plants & Trees)
Flora
(Flores, plantas y árboles)
Árbol de tabonuco
Tabonuco tree

Flora
(Flowers, Plants & Trees)
Flora
(Flores, plantas y árboles)
Árbol de caimito
Star Apple Tree

Flora
(Flowers, Plants & Trees)
Flora
(Flores, plantas y árboles)
Helecho gigante
Giant Fern

Tarántula marrón común de Puerto Rico
Common Puerto Rican Brown Tarantula

Mamíferos
Mammals

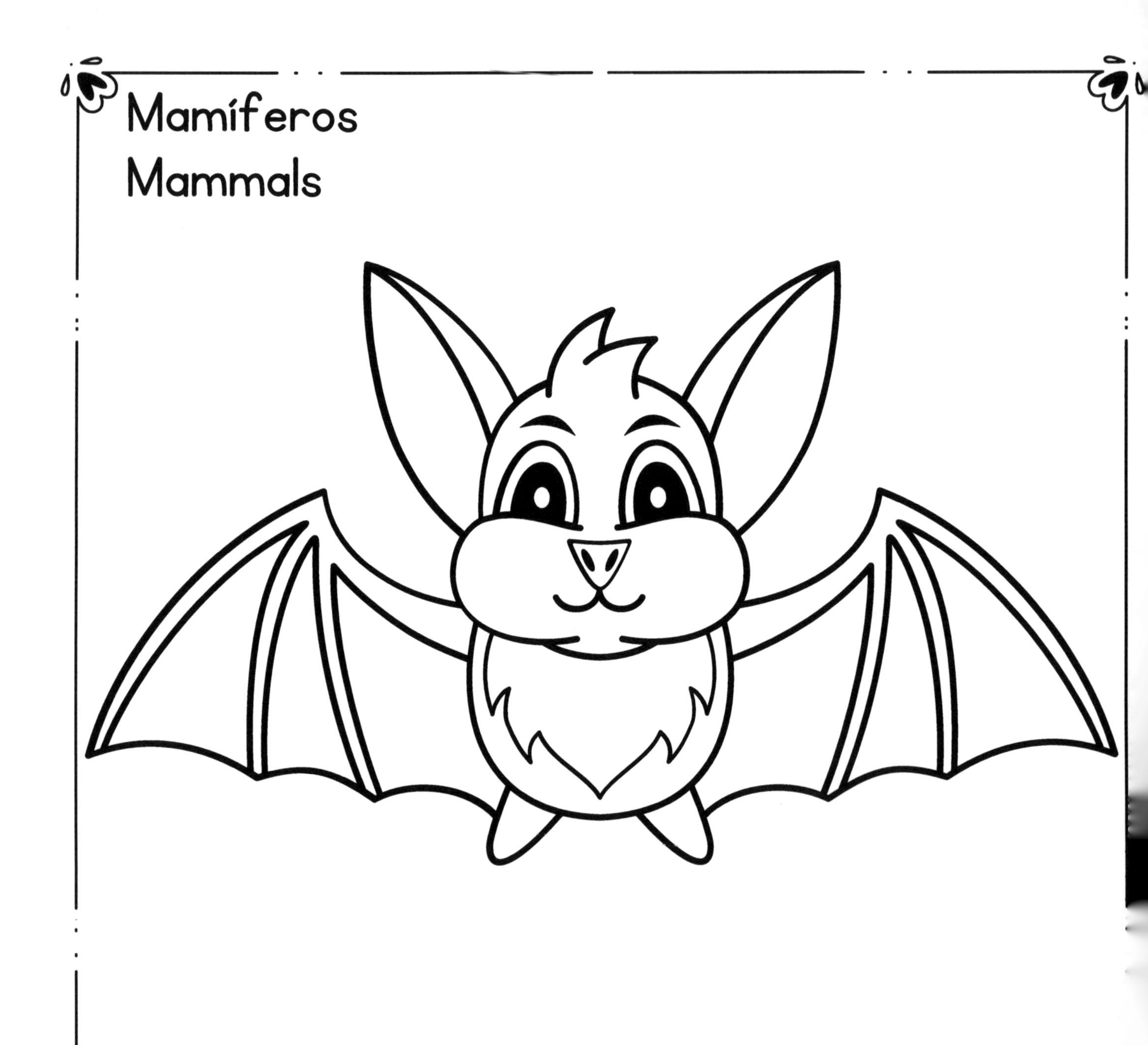

Murciélago Bigotudo Menor
Sooty Mustached Bat

Mamíferos
Mammals
Mangosta
Small Indian Mongoose

Especies
acuáticas
Aquatic
animals

Pez Espada
Green Swordtail

Especies acuáticas
Aquatic animals

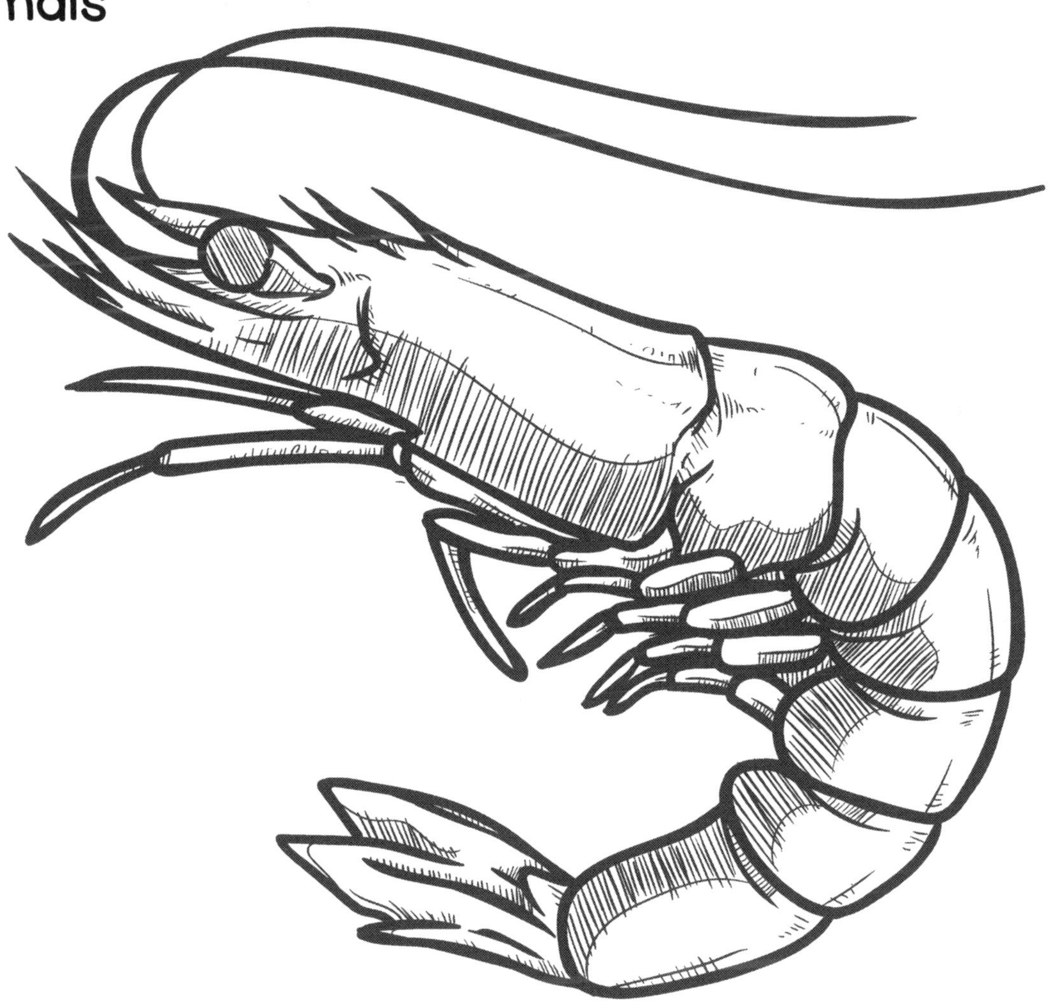

Camarón de río de garras grandes
Big-claw River Shrimp

Utiliza la cuadrícula para dibujar el otro lado de la cotorra y colorearlo.

Use the grid to draw the other side of the parrot and color it.

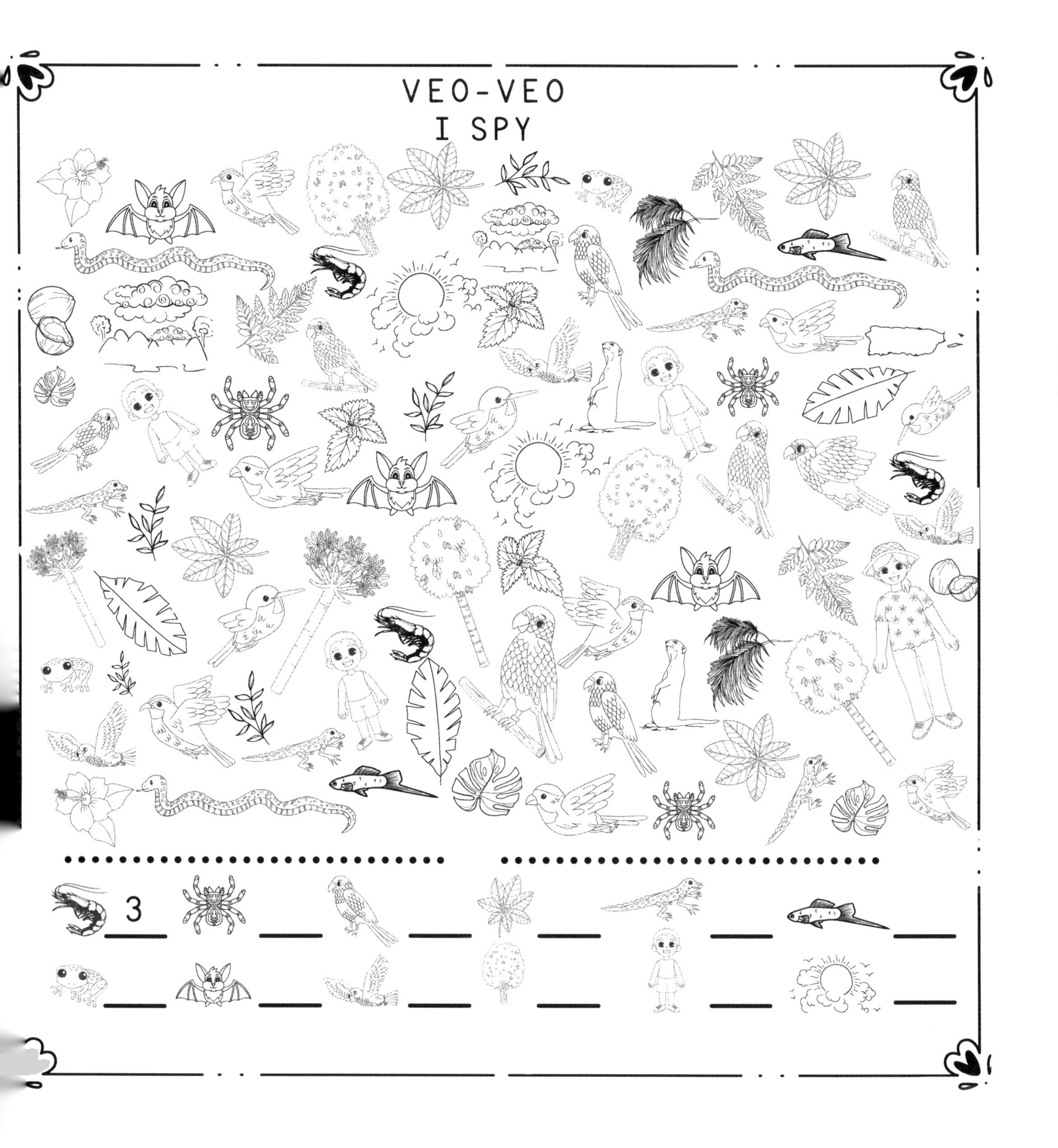
VEO-VEO
I SPY
3

Ayuda a Leo a encontrar las aves. Colorea todos las aves del sendero y tacha las que no son aves.

Help Leo find the birds. Color all the birds on the trail and cross out the ones that are not birds.

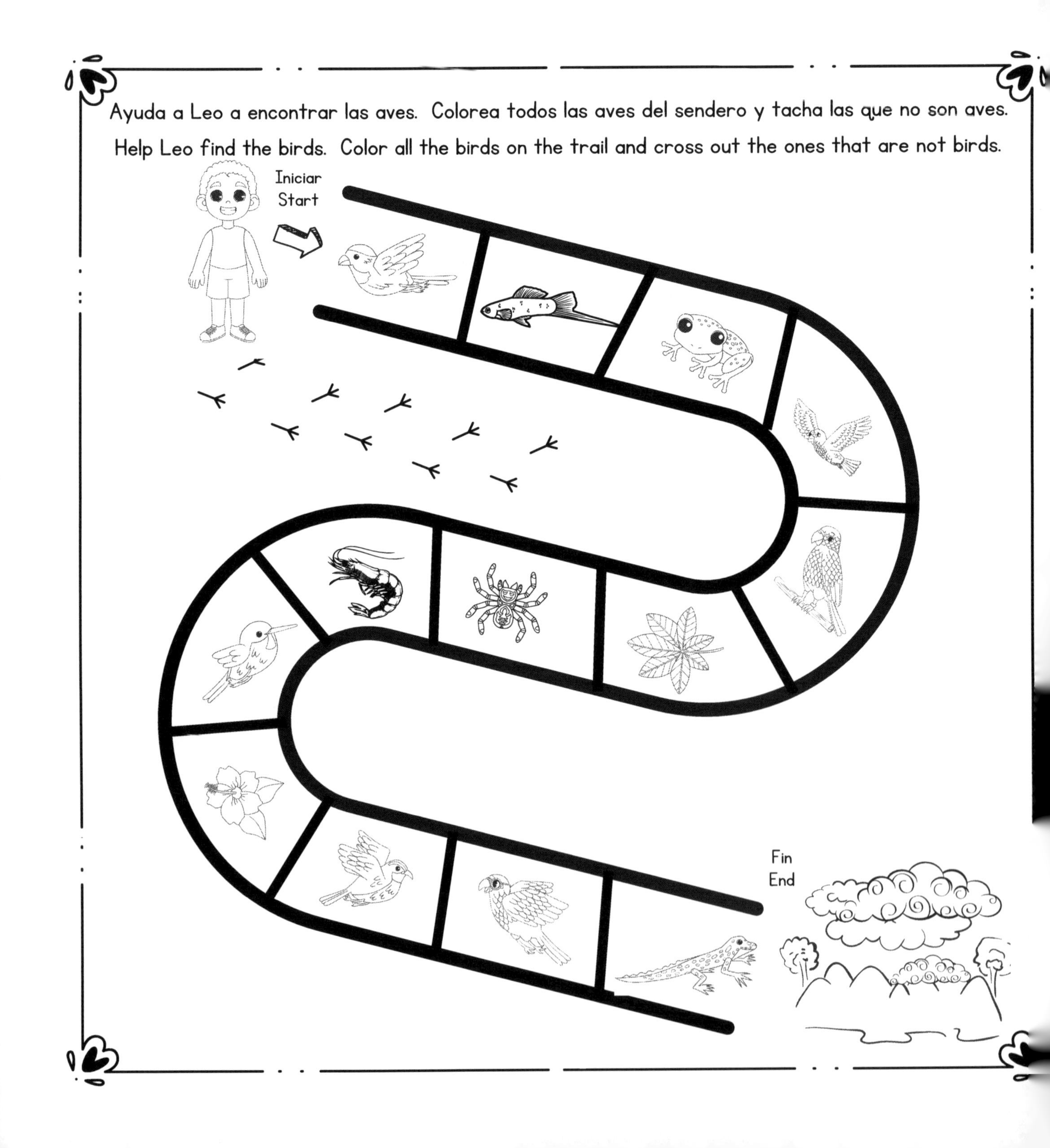

Suma el coquí en cada casilla y escribe tu respuesta después del signo de igualdad (=).

Add the coquí in each box and write your answer after the equal (=) sign.

+ = ______

+ = ______

+ = ______

+ = ______

+ = ______

Práctica de trazado
Tracing Practice

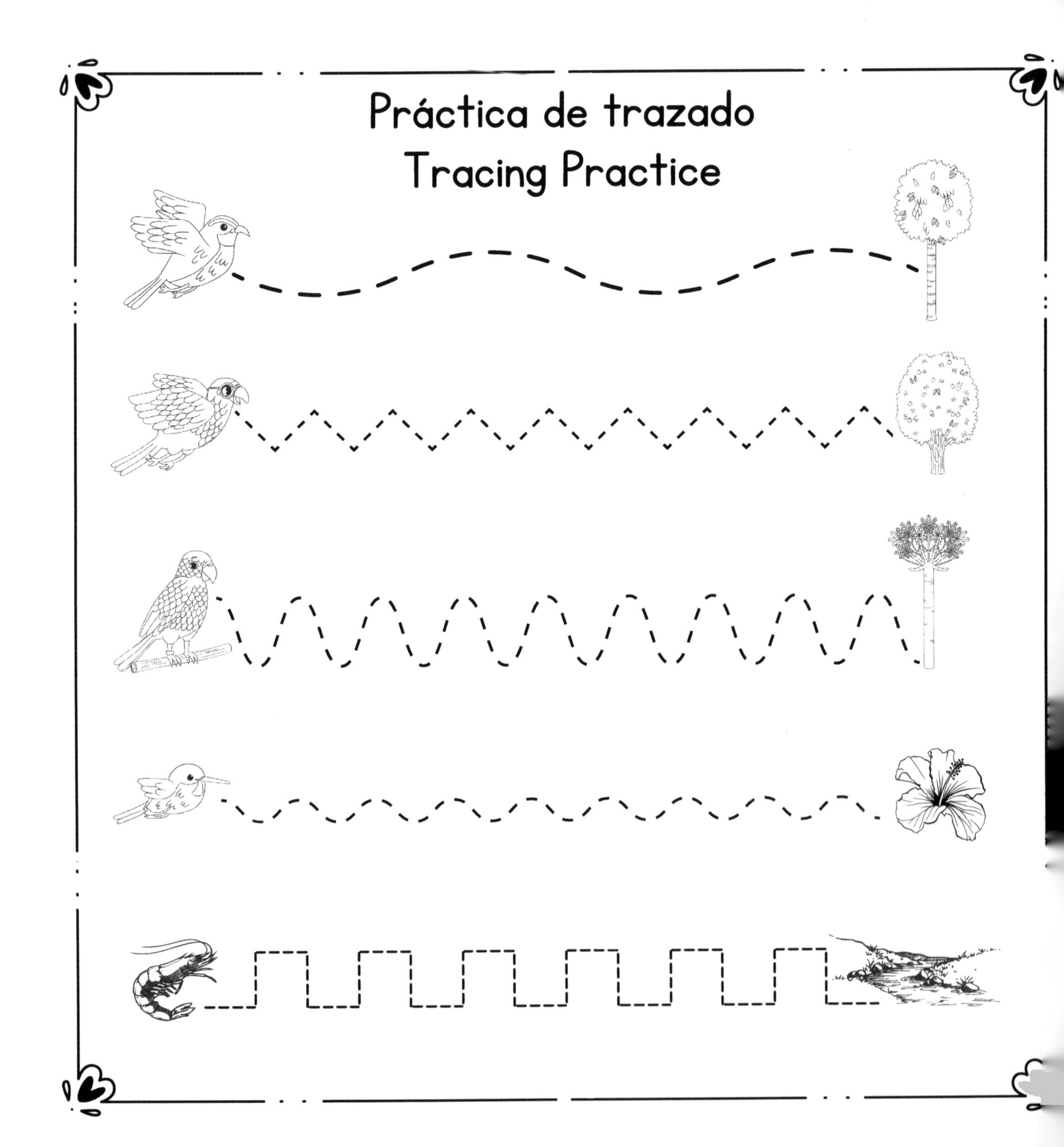

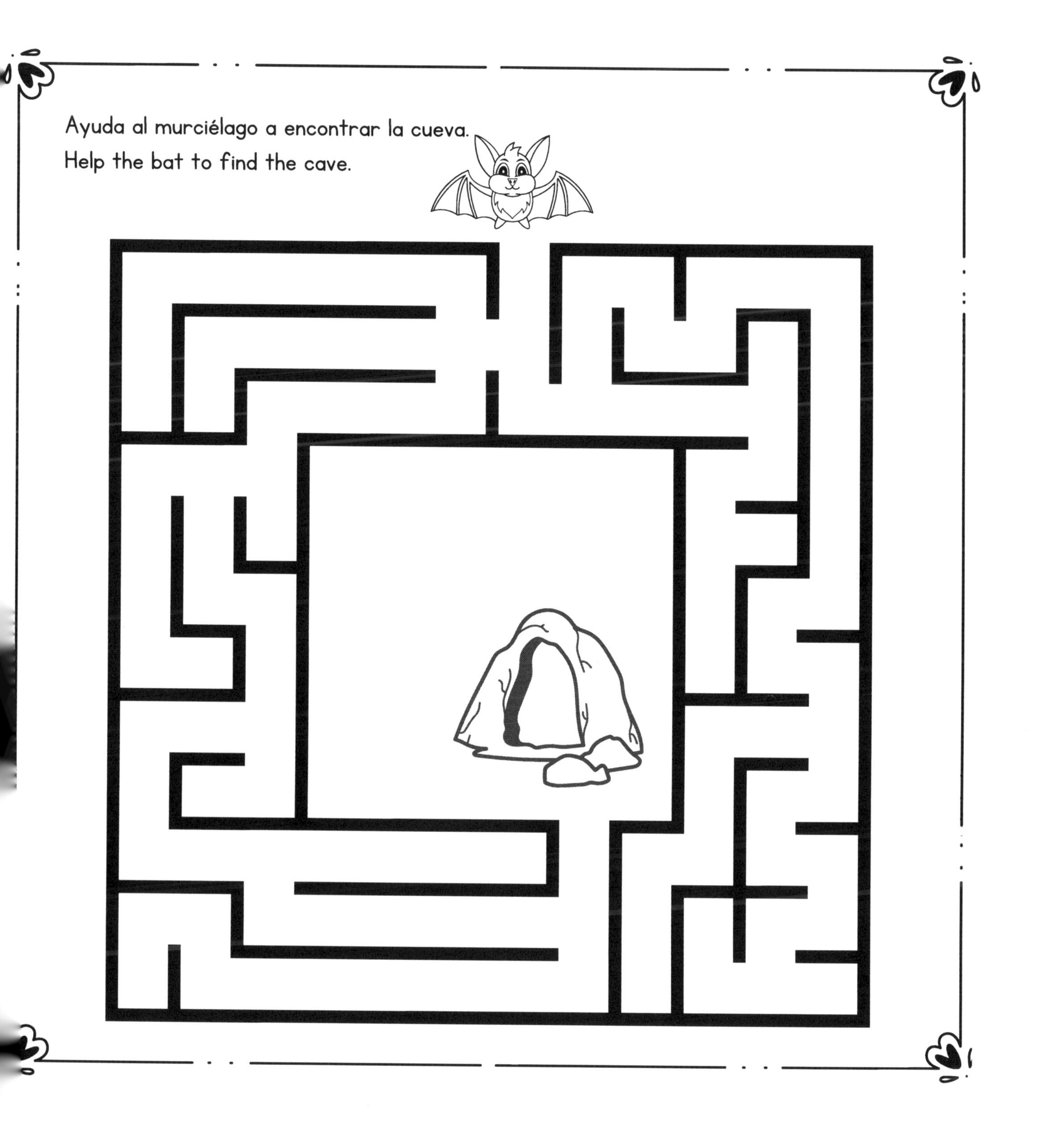
Ayuda al murciélago a encontrar la cueva.
Help the bat to find the cave.

Made in United States
Troutdale, OR
12/02/2024

25704497R00027